The
Bridie
Mae
Hayes

Henry
the Cat

Don't miss any of the Life and Times of
Birdie Mae Hayes!

The Gift
Henry the Cat

The Life and Times of

Birdie Mae Hayes

Henry the Cat

Jeri Anne Agee

Illustrated by Bryan Langdo

Sky Pony Press
New York

First Edition

This is a work of fiction. Names, characters, places, and incidents are from the author's imagination and used fictitiously.

Sky Pony Press books may be purchased in bulk at special discounts for sales promotion, corporate gifts, fund-raising, or educational purposes. Special editions can also be created to specifications. For details, contact the Special Sales Department, Sky Pony Press, 307 West 36th Street, 11th Floor, New York, NY 10018 or info@skyhorsepublishing. com.

Sky Pony® is a registered trademark of Skyhorse Publishing, Inc.®, a Delaware corporation.

www.skyponypress.com.

10 9 8 7 6 5 4 3 2 1

Library of Congress Cataloging-in-Publication Data is available on file.

Cover design by Sammy Yuen
Cover illustration by Bryan Langdo

Paperback ISBN: 978-1-5107-2456-3
Ebook ISBN: 978-1-5107-2461-7

Printed in Canada

Table of Contents

Chapter 1

THE INVISIBLE CAT

When I woke up on Saturday morning, I wasn't expecting to find a big white fluffy cat sitting outside my bedroom window. But there he was. He stared at me, then he yawned, laid down on the window ledge, and started cleaning himself. *Well, just make yourself at home why don't you!* I thought.

I got out of bed and went over to the window. I watched him through the glass for a few minutes, wondering if he might be one of the cats left over from when old lady Miller lived in the neighborhood. She had at least fifty cats before she moved away.

Mama stepped into my bedroom and said, "Good morning, Birdie Mae! What are you looking at out the window?"

I pointed to the cat and said, "Mama, it's the strangest thing . . . I woke up and this big white fluffy cat is just sitting right outside my window staring at me."

Mama looked toward the window and then walked over to get a better look. I noticed her back stiffen a little and when she turned around she had a funny look on her face. She came back and sat on my bed.

She looked right at me and said, "Birdie Mae, are you telling me there is a big white fluffy cat sitting outside your window, right now?"

"Yes ma'am! Isn't he the cutest thing?" I asked.

Mama still had that same funny look on her face. She said, "Now, I don't want to upset you, but Birdie Mae, I don't see a big white fluffy cat outside your window. Or *any* cat outside your window. But I do believe *you* see one. I think, though, you may be the only one who can see it." She paused. My mouth dropped open. "It sounds like I need to call Grandma Mae right away. I'll be right back."

And just like that Mama got up and left my bedroom in a hurry. I stared at the bedroom door and then back at the cat over and over again. I started getting a nervous feeling, and I knew this all had something to do with my gift—or what Mama now calls my "special abilities." That had to be the only reason Mama was calling Grandma Mae.

I could hear Mama talking on the phone but I couldn't hear what she was saying. Then, before I knew it, she was coming back down the hall. She rounded the corner to my room and said in a cheerful voice, "How about we take a ride out to Grandma Mae's house today?"

I immediately thought to myself, *Oh great . . . here we go again.*

Chapter 2

MY GIFT

I should probably back up a little bit and tell you how I got to this point in the first place, and exactly what my "gift" a.k.a "special ability" is. Don't get too excited. It's not a gift like a cool new bike or anything like that. It's something I was born with . . . my Grandma Mae has it too, and she calls it a fancy word—*clairvoyance*. I had to look that up in the dictionary. It kind of means someone who can see things before they happen—things in the future. Most people call it psychic. Basically, I can see visions of what's going to happen.

Not all the time—just some of the time—and that's the real frustrating part.

So anyway, my name is Birdie Mae Hayes and I'm eight years old and live in Rainbow, Alabama, with my Mama, Daddy, and my little brother Bubba. My best friend is Sally Rose Hope and we are in third grade. We've been best friends since we were born, which was in the same hospital, just one day apart, by the way. We've lived down the street from each other ever since. We hang out together every day except for when one of us is sick or something. But even then, we sometimes bring each other homework or soup. We definitely like the days when we bring soup better than the days when we bring homework.

You can probably imagine that I don't go around telling just anyone that I can see things before they happen. For one thing, no one would believe me, and for another thing, if they did believe me, they would probably try to make me prove it or something and that's just not how it works. Besides my family, Sally is the only other person who knows about my gift.

I found out about it a few weeks ago, after I had a vision of Doyle Baker falling out of a tree right before he did, and a vision of a fire in our backyard before it happened. That was the first time Mama and Daddy took me to visit with Grandma Mae about my special abilities. That was the first time she told me I was born with a gift.

It was a lot for a kid to take in all at once. Since then, I've really started noticing things, small things, and really paying attention to when I'm feeling strange. That's what happens before I see a vision—I start feeling strange and I get butterflies in my stomach. Last week it happened, and I knew which way Sally and I should go to avoid a big wasps nest with wasps swarming everywhere. And then the other day it happened, and I knew that if I didn't go upstairs with my little brother Bubba to start his bath water, he would overflow the bathtub.

Speaking of Bubba, that reminds me of the time he climbed out of his bed and decided to go dig in the garden in the middle of the night. I had a feeling so strong that night that it woke me up, and I had to wake up Mama and Daddy so they could go get Bubba out of the garden and give him a bath and put him back to bed. The next day we were all really tired. But Mama and Daddy were thankful that I had one of my feelings when I did, because who knows where he would have gone once he was done digging that big hole in the garden? Sometimes I'm surprised Mama ever lets that boy out of her sight.

But back to this whole cat thing—that's a new one for me, for sure. I don't know how I

feel about being able to see a cat that no one else can see. It seems like Mama isn't so sure about it either.

Chapter 3

VISIT WITH GRANDMA MAE

Later that day, when we pulled up to Grandma Mae's house, Grandpa was leaving, and he waved to us from his truck window. *Uh oh . . . It must be serious if Grandpa is leaving us alone,* I thought. Mama dropped me off and told me she would pick me up in a couple of hours after Grandma Mae and I had time to catch up on some things. By "catch up" I knew she meant "tell Birdie Mae why she's seeing an invisible cat."

Grandma Mae was waiting at the door when I walked up, and we waved goodbye to

Mama. Then Grandma Mae gave me a big hug and invited me in. We immediately went to the kitchen, where I could smell chocolate chip cookies. We sat outside on the back porch and quietly drank milk and ate cookies. The birds were chirping, the sun was shining, and I was happy to be sitting there with Grandma Mae, but I was ready to talk about why I was really there.

I was starting to get antsy, and really wanted to get some answers, when finally Grandma Mae said, "So tell me about this cat of yours that showed up out of nowhere."

I decided to just tell it like it happened. "Well, Grandma, this morning when I woke up there was a big white fluffy cat sitting outside my window. Mama came in and I tried to show her that he was sitting right there on the window ledge, but she couldn't see him at all . . . nothing . . . zilch. And now I don't know what to do or why he's there. I'm surprised anyone even believes me."

She said, "Of course we believe you. I think you are forgetting who you are talking to, my dear. Part of your gift is that sometimes you may be able to see things no one else can see. Sometimes it's a sign for you to pay attention and to be aware of your gift and your surroundings."

She looked down at me and smiled. Then she continued, "You see, Birdie Mae, when someone has a gift like we do, there is no end to the surprises that are in store for us in our lives. Like being able to see a cat that no one else can see. I think you are the lucky one here."

That's when I held up my hands and said, "Hold on just a minute, Grandma. Are you telling me I may be stuck with this cat that no one else can see?"

She took a big swig of milk and stuffed a cookie in her mouth. I could tell she was thinking it over. Hmm. Had I stumped Grandma Mae?

Finally, she smiled and said, "I rather like the thought of an invisible cat, don't you?"

"I guess so, Grandma. But why is he here? What does he want?" I asked.

She answered, "Sometimes animals or even people who have passed will show themselves to a person with a gift if there is still something in this world that they need to do. But they only seem to show themselves to someone with a very strong gift."

I just stared at her for a long time. So long that she ate another entire cookie while I was staring. So this cat had something it needed to do? What did that mean?

She could tell I was still a little bothered by having an invisible cat as a pet. She said, "You know, the reason you can see him may be that he needs your help. But I think it's up to you to figure out what he needs your help with."

"Okay Grandma, so let me get this straight. I've got this gift that lets me see things before they happen, but it depends on how closely I'm paying attention . . . and now you're telling me that an invisible cat may need my help, too?"

Grandma Mae was chewing her food and nodding her head like I'd just said the most normal things in the world.

"Would you like some more milk?" she asked.

I sighed and said, "Yes ma'am, I'm going to need some more milk, and please pass me the whole plate of cookies."

Grandma Mae laughed and said, "That's my girl, always up for an adventure!"

Chapter 4

HENRY THE CAT

After my visit with Grandma Mae, I didn't see the cat again until the next day. Sally and I were on the swings at the park in our neighborhood, and he strolled right up and started weaving in and out of my legs and purring up a storm. I froze for a second because I still wasn't convinced that *no one else* could see this cat but me. He was so real! I could feel his fur against my legs and hear his purring. But Sally was looking right at the ground, still babbling on about something that she watched on TV last night.

That's when I decided to find out for sure. Sally knows about my gift, so I figured this may not surprise her at all.

I turned to Sally and said, "Sally, what I'm about to tell you might be hard for you to believe, but you know how I can see things sometimes before they happen?"

Sally looked around to make sure we were alone and whispered, "Yes, you mean the feeling you get when you have butterflies in your stomach, and when you close your eyes you can see into the future?"

I glanced around too and whispered back, "Yes, that's right. Well, now I have a new thing to tell you about."

I took a deep breath and said, "I have a cat. Well, I sort of have a cat. I'm the only one who can see him. He showed up at my bedroom window yesterday morning. He was there plain as day, but Mama couldn't see him." The more I talked the crazier I sounded even to myself.

"So here goes nothing," I whispered. "Do you see a big white fluffy cat sitting right here by my feet?"

Sally stared at me with wide eyes. She looked at my feet, then back at my face, and said, "Nope, no cat there."

Then she started swinging in her swing again. Sally had a smile on her face. She shook her head from side to side and said, "Being your friend gets more interesting every day." And we both started laughing.

She said, "If you say there is a cat there, then I believe you. I just wish I could see him, too. You know how I love cats. I bet he's cute."

I filled Sally in on my day yesterday from the moment I woke up and first saw the cat to the visit with Grandma Mae. I even told her about the stomachache I had later after eating so many chocolate chip cookies. She listened to the story with her mouth hanging open most of the time—I thought a bug might fly in there if she didn't close it soon.

After I finished talking and she closed her mouth, she asked, "What do you think he wants? I mean, why do you think he's here? Does he have a name? Have you named him yet?"

Just as I was about to tell Sally to cool it with all of the questions, I saw that the cat was wandering away, down the path leading out of the park toward the neighborhood houses.

I stopped swinging and said, "He's leaving! And as far as a name goes, I've been thinking about it and I kind of think he looks like a Henry."

"Well, since I can't see him, Henry sounds as good a name as any. Where do you suppose he's going?" she asked.

I looked at Sally and said, "There's only one way to find out! Let's follow him! He may even want us to come with him."

We both hopped off our swings and ran after Henry the cat down the hill.

Chapter 5

LOST DOG

We followed Henry—well, I followed him and Sally followed me—for a few blocks. Then, out of nowhere, I started getting butterflies in my stomach. It was one of my feelings! I stopped and closed my eyes, and immediately I saw a vision of Peter Doolittle standing in front of his house, and he looked upset. We had to help him!

I told Sally that we needed to turn on the next street, to get to Peter's house. I wasn't sure what he was upset about, but that became clear pretty quickly. As we approached his house, there he was, standing out in front, frantically calling for Marshall, the Doolittles' little wiener dog. We also saw his little sister, Izzy, and his mother, and they were both calling for Marshall, too. Mrs. Doolittle seemed so nervous and worried.

She said, "Marshall never runs off like this. He's been gone overnight, and he has never done that before."

Sally and I agreed to help them search for Marshall. I still had a funny feeling and lots of butterflies in my stomach. When we were farther from Peter and his family I closed my eyes again and then I had a clear vision. I saw Marshall walking through a dark space with a low ceiling, and then crouching down, trembling and whining. It seemed like he might be under some sort of porch or in a basement of a house. The problem was, I wasn't sure which house!

Henry hadn't come into the Doolittles' yard with us. He stayed perched just outside of their yard, on the grassy lawn of the neighbor's house. He watched us for a few minutes and then let out a long meow. I froze and looked at everyone, but no one else appeared to have heard anything.

I started walking slowly toward Henry, with Sally following close behind. As I got closer to Henry, he jumped up and dashed toward the back of the neighbor's house. I hurried after him and Sally followed me while the Doolittles kept looking around their own yard. When we were out of earshot of the others, Sally whispered, "Are we following Henry right now?"

I said, "Yes, but I'm not sure where he's taking us."

She said, "Do you think he knows where Marshall is?"

"I don't know if he does, but I'm pretty sure I know. I think Marshall is under a house, but I don't know which one," I said.

Henry finally stopped when he reached the neighbor's backyard. He walked right up to the small closed door that leads to the crawl space under the house. He sat down and looked up at me and let out a long *meeoow*, then stood up and started weaving in and out of my legs. Was this the house Marshall was under? I wasn't sure how Henry knew this was the place, but I had a feeling he was right. I needed to make sure.

Sally and I must have had the same idea because we both put our ear to the door. We could hear a faint whining coming from inside. As soon as we heard it, we looked at each other with wide eyes. That had to be Marshall! We called out his name and then heard a weak bark. Sally ran around to the front of the house, waving madly and calling everyone over. As soon as Mrs. Doolittle realized what was going on, she ran over and knocked on the neighbor's front door. After a few minutes, Mrs. Doolittle and the neighbor came around the corner, and he opened the door. Marshall came running out, and boy did he stink! He smelled all musty, like an old pair of socks, and he was shaking. Peter picked up the little dog and he started wagging his tail and licking all over Peter's face.

Mrs. Doolittle said, "Birdie Mae and Sally, thank you girls so much for finding our sweet little Marshall!"

As we walked back to the Doolittles', Mrs. Doolittle told us that the neighbor had been having some work done on his house and had left the door that leads to the crawl space open for several hours. Marshall must have gone in during that time and probably fell asleep. By the time he woke up, the door was closed.

Mrs. Doolittle turned to Marshall and said in a baby voice, "Poor wittle baby, let's get inside and get you cleaned up and get some kibble in your tummy."

Peter's face turned bright red, and as they carried Marshall home we heard him say, "Mom, do you have to talk to the dog like that? It's embarrassing!" Sally and I both giggled and waved goodbye.

And then I remembered Henry. I looked around to see where he had gone, but he was nowhere to be found. I didn't know if he had just wandered off again, or if he had disappeared into thin air.

Chapter 6

SALLY'S BROTHER DARREL

After all the excitement at the Doolittles',
we decided to go to Sally's house for a little
while. On the way over I kept an eye out for
Henry while Sally talked about how cool it
was finding Marshall, and on and on about
"our" secret cat.

As soon as we headed up the driveway
to Sally's house, I saw Henry in their garage.
His big white fluffy body was sitting in the
box strapped to the front of Darrel's bicycle.
Sally's older brother Darrel is in fifth grade,
and he loves his bike. He rides it everywhere

and carries all sorts of stuff in the box tied
to the front like a basket. He's always finding
and bringing home animals in it, like lizards,
snakes, injured birds, even stray puppies. And
now Henry was in it!

Henry was giving himself a bath by licking a front paw and rubbing it across his face. I stopped as soon as I saw him, and Sally must have sensed something because she stopped too and said, "What's the matter? You see Henry, don't you? What is he doing?"

I answered, "Yes, he's in your garage sitting in the box on Darrel's bike!"

Sally and I ran up the driveway and into the garage. Henry ignored us and continued to clean his face. When we got a bit closer, he hopped out of the box and started circling around Darrel's bicycle. I looked at Sally and was just about to tell her that Henry was on the move again when I had another feeling like something was about to happen. I knew a vision was probably coming soon, I could just tell. I had never had any of my visions this close together. Did it have anything to do with Henry, or was it just a coincidence?

Just then, the door swung open and Darrel bounded out of the house fully decked out in his bike helmet, knee pads, and elbow pads. *It must be race day*, I thought. Darrel races his bike on some dirt tracks right outside of town, and he's really good at it.

He said, "Move it, girls, I've got a bike race to get to!"

At that moment, my feeling got even stronger. I closed my eyes, and saw a vision of Darrel riding his bike down the big hill in our neighborhood—and his back tire blowing out, causing him to go flying off the bike and rolling down the hill.

Suddenly, a loud *meow* right next to me startled me out of my vision. I opened my eyes and looked down, and there was Henry sitting right next to Darrel's bicycle's back tire. I bent over to get a better look and saw something shiny and silver sticking out. What was that? I leaned in closer and saw that it was a nail head.

That would cause his tire to blow! He was going to get hurt!

Darrel hopped on his bike but before he could pedal off I said, "Darrel, wait! There's a nail in your back tire!"

He jumped off the bike, looked at the tire, and yelled "DAD!"

Mr. Hope came out of the house and Darrel showed him the nail in his tire.

He said, "It's a good thing you saw this before the race. If you had been racing and this tire blew out, it could have been really bad."

Sally blurted out, "Birdie Mae noticed it first, so she basically saved his life!"

Mr. Hope said, "Well, that may be a little dramatic, but I do think she saved him from a possible accident. Thank you, Birdie Mae."

"Yeah, thanks Birdie Mae. That could have been bad," said Darrel.

I smiled and said, "You're welcome," and tried to keep an eye on Henry as he strolled down the driveway. He had showed me the nail! I wondered if I should follow him. I was almost ready for our adventures to be over for the day. If this kept up, I'd be saving animals and people all day, every day.

I decided not to go after Henry this time, and Sally and I headed back to the park. But as we were walking, I looked behind us—and there was Henry, following us from a distance.

Chapter 7

GRANDMA RAY

For the next couple of nights, Henry showed up outside my window, but I had not seen him around anywhere else since the day we found Marshall and helped Darrel with his tire. I was kind of glad to have a break, because I was starting to think that every time I saw him it meant that something was going to happen, and that meant I really should be on my game. And that takes a lot of focus.

But the more I thought about it, the more I thought that Henry was trying to get me to follow him somewhere. What if my visions had interrupted wherever it was he was trying to take me? As Grandma Mae said, maybe he needed my help, and that's why I could see him.

The other possibility was, what if I now *needed* Henry to be able to see my visions? I've been thinking about that since Henry showed up. I had so many visions that first day I saw him, and I haven't had any since. I'd even tried to have a few visions at school, but nothing happened. I really needed to talk to Grandma Mae again soon.

Peter told everyone at school how we found his dog, Marshall. And Sally told everyone at school how I saved her brother, Darrel. People kept coming up to me all day asking about it. I guess I was the news for the day. It must have been a slow day.

Even Virginia Flanker asked me about it, which is surprising since she pretty much hates me. Wait—Mama says I shouldn't use the word "hate"—so, what I meant to say was, I was surprised when Virginia asked me about it since she pretty much *dislikes* me. Virginia is tall and has long blond hair that she wears in a high ponytail on top of her head and she usually wears dresses to school. Mama says maybe she isn't very nice to me and Sally because she's jealous that we're friends with Peter Doolittle—she has a crush on Peter. Yuck!

But it's true. Everyone knows that Virginia Flanker likes Peter Doolittle because she doesn't try to hide it. One time she kissed him on the cheek at school! Double yuck! And, just like I told Mama, I don't know what she has against me and Sally because we have always been nice to her, even when she used to put salt in her hair and then suck it off. She still does it sometimes. She sucks on the end of her ponytail to get it wet and then takes the salt shaker and shakes salt all over the end of it and then sucks the salt off. Mama couldn't think of a thing to say when I told her about that.

Anyway, hearing everyone talking about Peter's dog reminded me of the time Billy's dog followed him to school and someone left the door open and he wandered in. Billy was already in class and the dog ran all over the school looking for him. When he finally found him, he jumped up on Billy's desk and licked his face clean and Billy's mom had to come and pick the dog up.

I guess if Henry decided to do that, no one else would see him! That would be kind of cool. I still wasn't sure I liked being the only one who could see him, though.

Later that week, I woke up one morning after dreaming about my Grandma Ray—though I couldn't remember much about my dream except that she was in it. She's my other grandma. I have a Grandma Mae and a Grandma Ray. It gets real confusing sometimes. Grandma Mae is the one who told me about my gift. She is my daddy's mama and I was named after her. Then I have my Grandma Ray, who is my mama's mama. She lives nearby too, but I hadn't seen her in a few weeks.

That morning, I woke up thinking about her. Usually, that would make me smile because I've learned all sorts of fun things from Grandma Ray. Things like: how to tell time, how to hula-hoop, how to belly dance, how to golf, how to bowl, how to play tennis, how to cross-stitch, how to pretend you didn't know you were speeding when the police pull you over, and lots of other cool stuff.

But that day, my dream about Grandma Ray left me with an uneasy feeling. I was really hoping it was just because I was hungry.

Chapter 8

THE WALK

After I ate breakfast, I noticed Henry sitting
outside my window. I opened it and let him
into the house for the first time. He just
purred and rubbed up against me and then
curled up on my bed and went to sleep.

Just then, the doorbell rang. I leaned out
my window and saw Sally on my front porch.
I left Henry on the bed and put my jacket
on and told Mama and Daddy goodbye. They
were busy chasing Bubba around trying to get
him dressed and ready to go with them to run
some errands. As usual, he was scampering

around the house in his underwear. This time
he was playing cops and robbers. He had a
mask over his eyes like a robber and a belt
around his waist with handcuffs and toy guns
in a holster. Sally and I had to laugh as we
closed the door and left for the park.

When we got to the bottom of the
driveway, I was surprised to see Henry waiting
there for us. I looked at him . . . and then back

at the house. A minute ago he was on my bed! How did he get here?

We turned toward the park, but Henry must have had other plans because he started walking in the opposite direction.

I told Sally about Henry, and we both agreed that we needed to follow him.

We walked behind him for a couple of blocks and Sally said, "This is fun! I wonder who we'll help today. Maybe we can be like a superhero team or something!"

I smiled at her and just shook my head. It did seem like it could be the start of an adventure, but I had an uneasy feeling. And it seemed to be getting worse.

Before Sally and I knew it, we had walked and talked so long that we had followed Henry out of our neighborhood and toward the train tracks. We then followed him along the train tracks—well, I followed him, and Sally kept asking me every ten seconds if he was still there. As we went farther on the tracks, the houses turned to farms, and fields of cotton stretched as far as you could see. We saw an old cotton gin in the distance, and it reminded me of the time Sally and I got to jump around in one of the big bins of freshly picked cotton.

Then it happened . . . the uneasy feeling I was having turned into a vision. When I closed my eyes, I saw Grandma Ray lying on the floor of her kitchen in the dark with groceries scattered everywhere around her. Was she hurt? I didn't know where Henry was taking us, but I knew that we had to get to Grandma Ray's house and fast. Maybe that's why she had been on my mind lately. I knew something must be wrong.

I told Sally that I'd just had one of my feelings and that we needed to hurry up. Just then, we came to the clearing behind my Grandma's house. I recognized it immediately. Had Henry been leading us here?

When we got to the backyard I could see Grandma Ray's car parked in the driveway with the trunk open. We walked a little closer and noticed that the screen door to the kitchen was cracked open. Henry had disappeared into the house.

I called out to Grandma Ray from the backyard, but there was no answer.

When we reached the back door, I yelled to her again. "Grandma, it's me, Birdie Mae."

Then we heard her voice call out, "Birdie Mae, I'm in the kitchen . . . I've fallen and I can't get up!"

We went inside, and I saw Grandma Ray lying on the floor, looking just like I'd pictured!

"Oh my gosh, Grandma! What happened?"

"I slipped when I was bringing in the groceries, and I think I may have broken my ankle. Thank goodness you came along when you did, or I may have been sleeping on the kitchen floor tonight." She laughed when she said it.

I was glad to see that Grandma still had her sense of humor, at least. But that would've been terrible for her!

I didn't know what to do at first, so I called Daddy. He said to sit tight and that he and

Mama would be there as soon as they could. Sally and I were too small to pick Grandma Ray up off the floor, so we sat down beside her while we waited for Mama and Daddy.

After about ten minutes they came running through the back door. Mama let out a loud gasp and ran over to Grandma Ray as she said, "Mama, what happened? Are you okay?"

Grandma said, "Well, don't just stand there asking me questions, help me up. I need a little help getting up off the floor. I do think I may have a broken ankle."

As Daddy picked Grandma up and carried her to the door, Mama was already on the phone with Dr. Roberts making arrangements for him to meet them at the doctor's office.

Sally and I could hear Grandma complaining about it the whole time Daddy carried her to the car. I wondered if Grandma Ray was afraid to go to the doctor like I am sometimes. Mostly I don't like it because I don't want to get a shot. Would Grandma Ray have to get a shot?

We ran to catch up with Daddy while Mama was still on the phone with the doctor. Neither one of us wanted to walk all the way back home, even if it did mean taking a trip to the doctor's office first. We sat in the backseat with Grandma Ray and she rested her legs across our legs. It reminded me of the first time I went to Birmingham, a few months ago.

I remember I couldn't believe my eyes when I saw all those tall buildings and cars and people everywhere. I might have seen more of it, but Grandma Ray had been in the backseat with me with her feet propped up on my legs then, too.

She kept saying, "Birdie Mae, look at my feet—look at the size of those things!" Mama had been taking Grandma Ray to the doctor to have some big bumps called "bunions" taken off her feet. Bunions rhymes with onions, that's the only way I can remember it. I don't know why Grandma Ray wanted me to look at them. Mama says when people get older they sometimes like to talk about everything that's wrong with them.

When we got to the doctor's office, a nurse came out with a wheelchair, and they took Grandma Ray into the building with Mama following close behind.

Daddy decided to take me and Sally home and then come back to get Mama and Grandma Ray. Once we were alone in the car with Daddy, he gave us the third degree about why we were all the way over at Grandma Ray's. Then he quickly realized maybe he didn't want to know all the details and said, "Oh never mind, it's just a good thing you came by to check on her!"

Sometimes Daddy forgets about my "special abilities," and then he remembers. Had Mama told Daddy about me being able to see an invisible cat? I didn't think now was a good time to bring it up.

On the drive home, I kept an eye out for Henry, but he was nowhere to be found.

Later that night Mama told me that Grandma Ray did break her ankle. She got a hot pink cast on it, and she wanted me to sign it the next time I was over there.

Chapter 9

FRIENDS AND AN INVISIBLE CAT

The following afternoon, Sally, Peter, Billy, and I met up after school at the neighborhood park at the top of the hill. Most afternoons we try to meet at the park because it's a pretty cool park and it's one of our favorite places. It also just happens to be conveniently located on the hill at the end of my street. From one side of the park you can look down and see all the houses in the neighborhood. From the other side, you can see a giant paper mill. Sometimes when the wind changes you can smell that paper mill for miles around and let me tell you it does NOT smell good.

At night, when it's all lit up, it looks like a big city. Sometimes Sally and I pretend it really is a big city and pick out which building we want to live in. Then we take turns thinking up what we want to be when we grow up. Sally can't decide between having a lemonade stand and driving an ice cream truck. I don't blame her, because those are both really good choices. Sometimes we decide that I'll do one and she'll do the other. But what I really want to do is ride on the back of one of those really big garbage trucks and jump off and on at each stop like the garbage men do. I don't know if I'll be able to do that *and* drive an ice cream truck, but I guess I can try.

We all took turns talking about what we wanted to be when we grew up. I knew Billy and Peter would say something about video

games and Ping-Pong. It seems like that's all they do when they are together.

Billy looked at Peter and said, "Did you hear about the Ping-Pong competition at school this year? We have one every year but I've never had anyone to enter it with before."

Peter answered, "Yes, I did hear about it. Let's do it! But we need to practice more."

Sally said, "Practice *more*? All you two do is practice Ping-Pong and play video games. I don't even know when you get your school work done. Also, you know who wins the competition every year? Doyle and Virginia. So, actually, you two better practice a lot so someone else can finally beat them."

Peter said, "You two should enter, too! What do you all think?"

I did not think that was a good idea! We were all talking about the Ping-Pong competition and how much practice Sally and I would need for it when I suddenly noticed a big white fluffy ball in the distance. It didn't take me long to figure out what it was. The longer I looked, the bigger it got, until it was clear that Henry the cat was heading our way. He was hard to miss, since his big white fluffy body stood out in the bright green grass he was walking through. I was still amazed that no one else could see him.

As soon as he reached us, he let out a meow and rubbed up against my leg. I looked around to see if anyone noticed, but no one

seemed to see or hear him, as usual. I feel
bad for not petting him, but if I did, it would
look extra weird. I was happy to see him, but
also a little nervous, as you can imagine. It
seems when Henry is around, some kind of
adventure is also right around the corner.

I kept an eye on him as we left the swings to
sit in the grass. He finally walked over and sat
down right in the middle of the four of us. Then
he started to groom himself until there couldn't
have been a spot he didn't clean. I tried not to

stare at him since no one else could see him, and I really tried not to yell out "THERE'S AN INVISIBLE CAT SITTING RIGHT HERE IN FRONT OF US, LICKING HIS BEHIND!" because I knew they would all think I was crazy.

I was just starting to relax and think that maybe Henry was just there for a visit when he stood up and started strolling down the hill back toward the neighborhood.

I knew this may be my only chance to find out where Henry was going, and I didn't want to waste any time. So I stood up and asked, "Who wants to go for a walk?"

Sally looked at me and mouthed the word "Henry?" I nodded my head and she understood that we needed to go. We really do need to come up with a code word.

Peter and Billy both agreed, too, and we set out on what I assumed was about to be some kind of adventure.

Chapter 10

THE JOURNEY

I couldn't figure out where Henry was leading us, and I wasn't having one of my feelings. I tried to relax and let the feeling come to me, but nothing was happening.

As we continued to walk through the neighborhood, I took a few deep breaths and looked around at the streets lined with magnolia trees and blossom trees with the smell of honeysuckle and roses in the air. I could hear kids playing and dogs barking and lawn mowers mowing. I've always loved roaming through the neighborhood because of all these things. That day, I might have enjoyed it more if I wasn't so busy following an invisible cat and trying to convince my friends to keep walking.

As soon as we reached the main entrance and turned left out of the neighborhood, Peter suddenly stopped and said, "How far are we going to go? I've got to be home for dinner by six o'clock."

Billy stopped too, and said, "Me too. Plus, I've got homework to do."

I froze mid-stride. Not because Peter had to be home for dinner at six o'clock, and not because Billy had homework to do. I froze because I suddenly knew where we were going. I closed my eyes and could see it plain as day: Henry the cat looking up at me, right by the dumpster behind what was clearly Daddy's store! I didn't say anything to anyone about the vision I just had because I wanted to keep it to myself until I was sure about why we were going to Daddy's store. And I didn't want Peter and Billy to think I was crazy.

I had to come up with a good reason for everyone else to keep walking, because I wasn't about to turn around now.

I quickly said, "I thought we could walk over to Daddy's grocery store and get a cookie!"

As soon as I said the word "cookie," they were all in. My friends know what the cookies at Daddy's store are like. They are about as big as your head and have extra chocolate chips in them. They are so good! Daddy says people come from miles around just for those cookies.

Daddy's store isn't the shortest walk, and we hadn't told any of our parents where we were going. I was starting to get nervous about walking this far, but I knew we had to make it to Daddy's store. I sped up when I noticed it was starting to get dark, and because I was getting nervous the closer we got. It seems like every time I have a vision, something or someone needs my help. This time, I worried that Henry needed my help— but I didn't know why, just that we had to get to Daddy's store. Henry must have sensed what I'd seen because he stopped, looked at me, and meowed as if to say "hurry up."

We still had a good bit of ground to cover before we got to Daddy's store. I couldn't believe everyone was still with me the farther we walked. They must really like Daddy's cookies.

Chapter 11

SURPRISE FOR FOUR

As the sky turned darker, it started getting a little cooler outside. Henry stayed a good bit in front of us, but I made sure not to take my eyes off him.

Soon, I began having another one of my feelings. I closed my eyes for a second and felt the butterflies in my stomach, but there was no vision along with it. I stopped to catch my breath and closed my eyes for even longer, but still there was nothing.

I thought about Grandma Mae and what she would tell me. She would tell me to relax my mind and my body and let any thoughts come to me, and all of that stuff that is hard for a kid to do.

But I really wanted to try. I closed my eyes one more time and I saw it. Clear as a bell, I saw where I was supposed to go, and why! My heart began beating a little faster and I opened my eyes and started walking a little quicker, and then running.

The others were still with me, and as we rounded the top of the hill, there was Daddy's store just on the other side of the street. We crossed the street and I ran behind the store, where all of the garbage dumpsters are kept and deliveries are made. That's where I'd seen Henry in my first vision. Sally, Peter, and Billy followed close behind. I headed into a wooded area near a creek back there. As soon as I reached the edge of the creek I saw them.

Four tiny kittens huddled together inside an old tire on the ground!

Henry was sitting right next to them. Were these Henry's babies? They had to be. One of the kittens was solid white, just like him. The other three kittens had different colored paws and a few colored markings on their ears or tails, but they still looked like Henry.

By then, my friends had caught up with me. Thankfully, no one asked why I had run over there like a crazy person. Then it dawned on me . . . what if the others couldn't see the kittens?

I looked at them and nervously opened my mouth to ask, "Does everyone see four kittens right in front of us?"

But just then Sally squealed, "Oh my goodness . . . kittens!" and reached out to pick up the one that was meowing the loudest.

I could hear the kitten purring in her arms from where I stood. I let out a sigh of relief and said, "I'm glad you can see them, too!"

Peter looked at me in a weird way and said, "Of course we can see the kittens. We aren't blind, Birdie Mae!" and he elbowed me in the side and laughed.

Billy and Peter each reached down to pick up one of the little fur balls, too. The one Billy reached for was small and quiet compared to the others, and the one Peter picked up had orange ears and orange feet. The last one left was the solid white one that looked just like Henry. I picked him up, and he nuzzled my neck and purred. I didn't think I could be any happier than I was at that moment.

Then I looked down and there was Henry weaving in and out of my legs as if to say *Thank you, thank you,* over and over again.

When he finally walked away, I watched him climb to the top of the dumpster and perch on top of a box like he was king of the world. I smiled at the sight.

I kept my eye on Henry as I held his tiny little fur ball baby in my hands. Henry seemed so content that he was now lying down and cleaning himself again.

I gazed down at the tiny kitten in my hands and couldn't believe how much he resembled Henry. When I looked up, Henry was gone.

I wondered, *Could this be why Henry came to me?* If these were his kittens, where was the mother cat? I had so many questions, and no one to ask. I thought to myself that a trip to Grandma Mae's house might be in order. Maybe she could help shed some light on this whole situation.

But right then, I knew that those kittens needed a home. I handed Sally the white kitten I was holding and ran inside to get Daddy. When I reached the store entrance, the smell of cookies hit me and it made my stomach growl. I found Daddy right away, and he followed me outside with a worried look on his face.

As soon as Daddy saw those four fur balls he let out a long low whistle and asked, "Well, what do we have here?"

All four of us at once excitedly asked, "Can we keep them? Can we keep them?" and Daddy let out a big belly laugh.

He said, "Are you sure the mama cat isn't around here somewhere?"

I looked at Daddy and, in a whisper, I said what I believed to be true. "I don't think they have a mama or a daddy anymore."

He looked at me, but he didn't question it.

I knew that the kittens were Henry's and I knew that there was no mother cat coming back.

Daddy mentioned that the kittens looked hungry, and as if they understood, they each meowed their own different sweet sound.

He said, "Stay right here. I'll be right back."

Soon Daddy came back carrying a box with a baby's blanket in it, and a can of cat food.

After I asked Daddy for about the tenth time if we could keep them, he at least agreed to go inside and call everyone's parents and explain the situation. And to let them know

where we were, since it was now dark and
way past time for us to have been home.

A few minutes later, he pulled the car
around back and told us to hop in and bring
the kittens. Sally and I jumped up and down
and squealed with delight as we all climbed
into Daddy's car.

Chapter 12

LITTLE HENRY

We drove straight to our house because Daddy said everyone's parents were going to pick them up there. Sally's, Peter's, and Billy's parents had all agreed to take a look at the kittens. I knew that once they saw them we would all get to keep them. Everyone's family already had pets—Peter has Marshall, Billy has a dog that came to school that one day, Sally has a guinea pig, and my family used to have a dog but he ran off with the neighbor's dog one summer. (Sally and I used to say they ran off to get married.) None of us had ever had a cat before, but that was about to change.

When we got inside, Bubba went crazy once he saw the kittens.

He started yelling "Kitty, kitty, kitty, kitty!" and doing a dance around the room fully decked out in his new cowboy costume that mama had bought him. Buying costumes has been one way that Mama can get Bubba to wear more than just his superhero underwear.

After Daddy looked at each kitten carefully, he announced that there were three girls and one boy, and if everyone's parents agree to keep a kitten, then we better start picking out which one we want.

We all knew which one we wanted. The same kitten we had each picked up back at the store. It was easy. The small, quiet kitten went to Billy, the long-legged kitten with the orange paws and orange ears went to Peter, and the little kitten that was white with gray paws and meowed all the time went to Sally. That left one kitten: mine. It was the only all-white kitten and the only boy, and I was so excited that I got to keep the one that looked just like Henry! We each picked up our kitten and nuzzled it and then watched them play with each other.

"What should we name them?" Sally asked.

I looked at the white fluff ball in my arms and the big blue eyes staring back at me and said, "I think you look just like a Henry."

Everyone laughed, and Sally gave me a knowing smile. Of course, no one else but me knew what the real Henry looked like and how much this kitten resembled him. But my friends agreed that he looked like a Henry, and the name was chosen.

Sally stroked her kitten and said, "I think I'll call her Cotton because she looks like a puffy ball of cotton."

Billy and Peter were still trying to figure out what to name their kittens, especially since they both had girl cats. They wanted names that weren't too girly but still sounded cool.

Sally and I giggled at the two boys trying to come up with girl names. Then the doorbell rang and there were Sally's parents standing at the door with a box in their hands and big smiles on their faces.

When Peter's parents and Billy's parents arrived, they took one look at the kittens and both agreed to keep them. We were all so excited!

After everyone had gone and it was just me and Mama in the living room playing with little Henry, I said, "Do you think we could take him to see Grandma Mae soon?"

Mama gave me her understanding smile and said, "I think that can be arranged. I'll go call her now so she will know when to expect us."

Chapter 13

ANOTHER VISIT WITH GRANDMA MAE

The next afternoon, we put little Henry in his box and loaded it into the car to go to Grandma Mae's house. I had a lot of questions for Grandma Mae that I hoped she could answer.

I hadn't told Mama the details, but she knew that I wanted to talk to Grandma Mae about everything that went on with big Henry. I hadn't seen him since we found the kittens. Had he disappeared forever?

We drove to Grandma Mae's house with little Henry. He softly meowed. I knew Grandma Mae would go crazy over him, and she did.

Mama stayed and we all played with the kitten for a little while. Then Mama left and took little Henry back home so Grandma Mae and I could talk.

I said, "Grandma, so many things have happened over the past few days that I don't know how I'm feeling about all of it."

Grandma hugged me before we sat down and she said, "Tell me all about it."

I told Grandma about the crazy things that had been happening with my gift lately. How I helped find the Doolittles' dog Marshall, and how there was a nail in Darrel's tire, and about Grandma Ray falling and breaking her ankle, and of course about finding the kittens.

Then I explained the most important part: how Henry was there with me each time I'd had a vision, and that I'd had more of them than usual when he was around. That's what I was so confused about. Was Henry related to the visions?

"What if Henry is the reason I was having so many visions and now that he's gone, I may not have them anymore?" I asked Grandma.

Grandma Mae just smiled and said, "There's all kinds of ways to use your gift, Birdie Mae, but I don't believe that relying on an invisible cat is one of them. You may think you couldn't have done it without Henry, but if you really think about it, my guess is Henry just happened to be there when you had your visions."

I must have looked doubtful because Grandma Mae continued. "From what you told me, Sally was also there for all your recent visions," she said, "and several other things probably happened the same every time. Maybe you were always in your neighborhood, or at the park, or at your house. But I can promise you there is no one thing that is causing you to have your visions. It's just the gift you were born with."

That made sense. I hadn't thought about it that way. That still left one question, though.

I said, "But what about Henry? He's gone now and we have his kittens. Do you think that is why he showed up here?"

She said, "Yes, I think Henry was here for you and for those kittens. I don't know what happened to the mother cat, but it's clear that Henry knew these kittens needed caring for and he led you to them because he knew you would take care of them. And that's what you did. That may be all he wanted, and he may not be back."

That made me a little sad. I said, "Just as I was getting used to the big white fluffy guy, he disappears."

Grandma Mae said, "But look at what he gave you in return. Not only did you get more practice with your visions, but now you also have a beautiful little kitten!"

I smiled and jumped up and hugged Grandma Mae. "Grandma, you always know the right things to say to make me feel better."

She said, "I bet I know something else that will make you feel better. How about we go get some ice cream and then I'll drop you off at home so you can play with your new kitten?"

I said, "Now you're talking!" and we both laughed.

Chapter 14

ONE SPECIAL KITTEN

Over the next few days, there was still no sign of big Henry. I guessed he really was gone for good. I also hadn't had any visions since the last time I saw him.

Meanwhile, Sally, Peter, Billy, and I were all having fun with our new kittens, who were growing quickly into big fluff balls just like big Henry. There wasn't much else we talked about when the four of us were together, and we took turns sharing the funny things that our kittens did.

Sally told us how her kitten Cotton and the guinea pig weren't so sure about each other at first but now they seem to be friends.

Peter said, "I've never heard of a cat and a guinea pig being friends, but I guess there's a first time for everything!"

Then, one afternoon when I was lying on the bed petting little Henry, I had one of my feelings again! My stomach fluttered, and I felt very uneasy. I looked around, half expecting to see big Henry sitting outside my window again, but he wasn't there.

Just then, little Henry jumped off the bed and stood by my bedroom door. He looked up at me and meowed a tiny but long meow. I wondered if he might be hungry, so I got up and followed him down the hall. He continued to look back at me and meow as I followed him.

My strange feeling was getting stronger, and then it happened: I closed my eyes and I saw

the reason for my feeling . . . a vision of Bubba
climbing up the bookcase in the living room!

As soon as I opened my eyes, I ran toward
the living room and yelled out, "Mama, Bubba
is climbing on the bookcase again!"

When I rounded the corner into the living
room, I saw Bubba halfway up the bookcase
and little Henry pacing back and forth at the
bottom of it, meowing and meowing.

Just then Mama came into the room. She
paused for a moment in shock and then

hurried over and reached up to grab Bubba before he could get any higher. He was giggling and kicking his feet as she picked him up.

Mama put him down and said, "Bubba, how many times do I have to tell you not to climb on the bookcase? It's very dangerous and you could fall and hurt yourself."

Bubba looked at her for a few seconds like he was really thinking about something, and then held up three fingers and said, "Freee, you haff to tell me freee times." And he smiled a mischievous smile and ran over to his toy chest and started playing with his army men like nothing at all had happened.

Later that afternoon, I was swinging in the hammock in the backyard thinking about what had happened earlier, and how I had the feeling and then the vision of Bubba on the bookcase. I was glad I still had my gift, even if it was stressful sometimes! But something kept nagging at me, and I wasn't sure what it was.

Then I realized what was bothering me. It was little Henry. Did he know that Bubba was climbing on the bookcase, too? Was he trying to lead me to him and I had the vision at the same time?

I didn't know for sure, but with a father like big Henry, I knew little Henry probably was not just any ordinary cat. I smiled to myself, thinking about the possibility of having another "special" cat. Thank goodness he wasn't invisible!

As if I had called his name, he pounced over to the hammock and hopped up into my lap, then licked my hand and curled up and fell asleep, purring.

I whispered, "Little Henry, I think you and I are going to have some adventures together."

And then I closed my eyes and let the swaying of the hammock drift me off to sleep.

Don't miss Birdie Mae Hayes's first adventure!

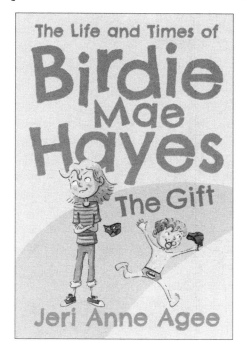

The Life and Times of

Birdie Mae Hayes

The Gift

Jeri Anne Agee

The Gift

Lately, Birdie Mae Hayes can't stop feeling like something is about to happen. Then she starts *seeing* things happen—before they happen! Birdie doesn't know if she's ready to take on the responsibility of this "gift." But one thing's for sure: life is going to be real interesting from now on!

ABOUT THE AUTHOR

Jeri Anne Agee grew up in Huntsville, Alabama, and graduated from the University of Alabama with a bachelor's degree in communications. An avid reader and a mother of three, Jeri Anne retired early from the financial industry, and at the age of forty-four, began writing her first children's book. Her quest to combine her own stories of growing up in the South with a character who is strong, lovable, loyal, and funny resulted in Birdie Mae Hayes. Jeri Anne currently resides in Franklin, Tennessee, with her husband, three children, and four rescue dogs.

ABOUT THE ILLUSTRATOR

Bryan Langdo spent his childhood drawing dragons and ninjas on whatever was around—sketchbooks, math tests, desks. He studied under author/illustrator Robert J. Blake, and then at the Art Students League of New York, where he focused on life drawing and portrait painting. After that he earned a BA in English from Rutgers College. Bryan is the illustrator of over thirty books. His picture book *Tornado Slim and the Magic Cowboy Hat* won a 2012 Spur Award for Storytelling from Western Writers of America. In addition to his work as an illustrator and writer, he works as an editor for an ESL website and app. Bryan lives in Hopewell, New Jersey, with his wife and two children. When not working, he likes to be in the woods.